To Jada, Jamaica, and Jessamine

Library of Congress Cataloging-in-Publication Data:
Kelley, True. Day-care teddy bear / by True Kelley. p. cm.—(A Just right book) SUMMARY: After building a tower,
finger-painting, and hearing a story, Anna and her teddy bear discover that day care is not so frightening after all.
ISBN 0-394-84305-3 (trade); 0-394-94305-8 (lib. bdg.) [1. Day care centers—Fiction. 2. Fear—Fiction. 3. Teddy bears—
Fiction] I. Title. II. Series: Just right book (New York, N.Y). PZ7.K2824Day 1990 [E]—dc20 88-43280

Manufactured in the United States of America 1 2 3 4 5 6 7 8 9 0

JUST RIGHT BOOKS is a trademark of Random House, Inc.

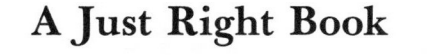

A Just Right Book

Day-Care Teddy Bear

By True Kelley

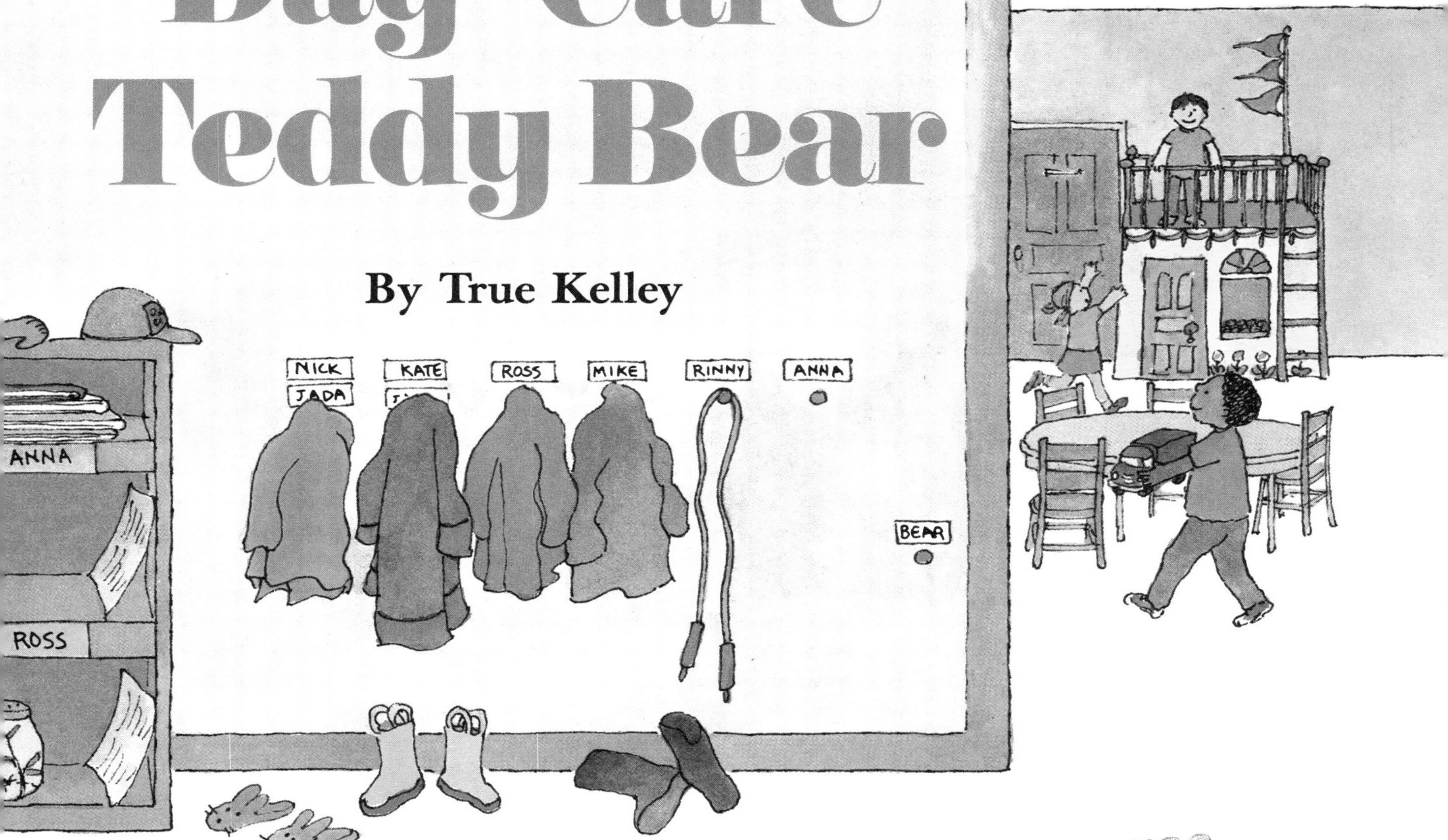

Random House New York

Published in the United States by Random House, Inc., New York, and simultaneously in Canada by Random House of Canada Limited, Toronto.

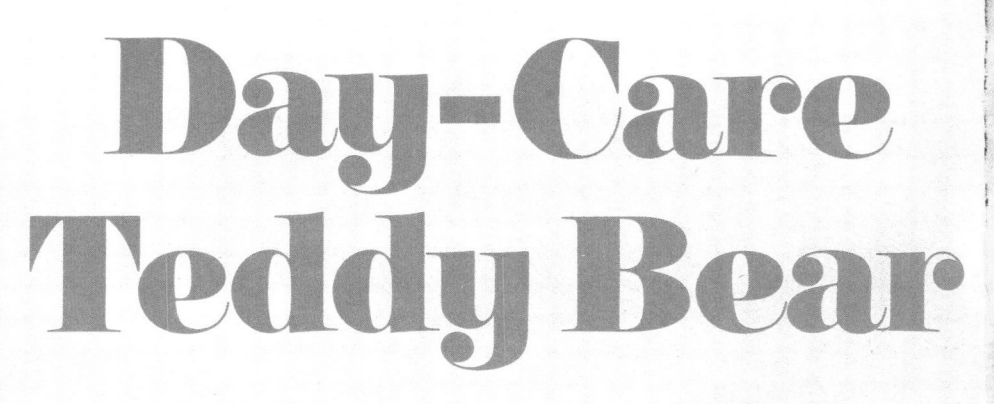

Today is Anna's first time at day care. It's her teddy bear's first time too.

Mrs. Johnson shows Anna her cubby. She helps Anna hang up her jacket and put away her backpack.

"Bear did NOT want to come to day care," says Anna.

"Maybe he'll change his mind," says Mrs. Johnson.

Mrs. Johnson shows Anna and her dad around the day-care room. The children are playing and having a great time.

"Here's the playhouse," says Mrs. Johnson.

"This is our art corner."   "This is the bathroom."

"Here's the dress-up corner."

"And this is Peanut Butter, the guinea pig."

"I have to go now, Anna," says Dad. "But I'll see you soon, when I come to pick you up."

"Need a hug," whispers Anna. "And Bear needs one too."

All the children are busy with dolls and blocks and cars and animals. Anna holds her teddy bear close. She's feeling shy.

"Maybe you'd like to help Ross build a tower," Mrs. Johnson says.

Anna helps Ross make the tower taller.
Ross is very good at sharing the blocks.

Suddenly the tower wobbles
and falls over!

Anna laughs. "Maybe next time
we should build a safe little house
for Bear."

Now it's circle time. All the children sit on the rug with Mrs. Johnson. Anna holds Bear on her lap. They talk about what they'll do today. Then they all sing some songs. Kate sings too loud!

Finger painting! Everybody loves that. The children put on smocks, roll up their sleeves, and go to it. They swirl the gooey paint around on the wet paper. Anna loves how it feels. She makes a picture of Bear. Maybe Dad will hang it on the refrigerator when they get home.

Look at Bear's paw painting!

What great pictures! What a great mess! Everyone helps clean up. Then the children wash their hands. Bear needs a bath!

It's snack time. Mrs. Johnson cuts an apple so everyone can see the star inside.

The children go outside to play.
Rinny blows bubbles, and Mike tries to catch them. Kate likes the swings best. Ross likes the slide. Anna is a little afraid to try the slide. Instead, she decides to work in the sandbox with some of her new friends.

Look! That silly Ross goes down the slide upside down.

Oh! Bear can do that too!

Lunchtime!

"Let's practice our good manners," says Mrs. Johnson.

Ross needs a lot of practice! But Bear's manners are perfect.

After lunch Anna and Ross play dress-up. Mike and Kate play a game. Rinny does a puzzle. But Nick is feeling sad. Anna lets him hold Bear.

"Quiet time," says Mrs. Johnson.
The kids get their mats and animals and blankets.
Anna feels very sleepy. She thinks Bear must be sleepy
too. Ross is not sleepy. He is very wiggly!

Wake up! It's story time.

Mrs. Johnson reads a book about babies.

Pay attention, Rinny. You'll have a new baby sister
or brother soon.

It looks as if Bear is still asleep. Wake up, Bear!

After the story Mike feeds the turtles and the fish. Anna, Ross, Nick, and Rinny make pretend food with clay.

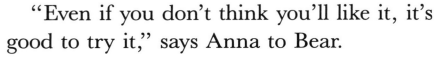

"Even if you don't think you'll like it, it's
good to try it," says Anna to Bear.
Bear gets a little of everything.
"He likes the blueberry muffins best,"
says Anna.

Just then Dad comes to pick up Anna. Anna pretends she doesn't see him. She's too busy.

"Anna, your dad's here," whispers Kate.

"Bear doesn't want to go home!" says Anna.

"I thought he didn't want to come to day care," says Dad.

"He changed his mind," Anna says.

"I sure missed you today," says Dad.

Dad loves Anna's picture! He holds Bear while
Anna puts on her jacket. Anna waves good-bye to
her new friends.

"Good-bye, Anna," says Mrs. Johnson. "Be sure
to bring our day-care teddy bear back tomorrow."

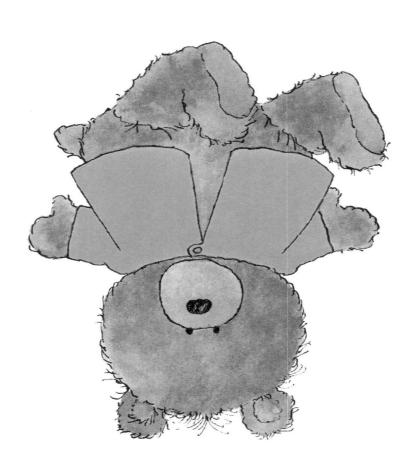